CHOOSE YOUR OWN ADVENTURE® · 33

THE DRAGONS' DEN

BY RICHARD BRIGHTFIELD

ILLUSTRATED BY PAUL ABRAMS

An Edward Packard Book

BANTAM BOOKS
TORONTO · NEW YORK · LONDON · SYDNEY · AUCKLAND

RL 5, IL age 10 and up

THE DRAGONS' DEN
A Bantam Book / June 1984

*CHOOSE YOUR OWN ADVENTURE® is a registered trademark of
Bantam Books, Inc. Registered in U.S. Patent and Trademark
Office and elsewhere.*

Original conception of Edward Packard

Front cover art by Paul Granger.

ISBN 0-553-24249-0

Published simultaneously in the United States and Canada

---

*Bantam Books are published by Bantam Books, Inc. Its trade-
mark, consisting of the words "Bantam Books" and the por-
trayal of a rooster, is Registered in U.S. Patent and Trademark
Office and in other countries. Marca Registrada. Bantam
Books, Inc., 666 Fifth Avenue, New York, New York 10103.*

PRINTED IN THE UNITED STATES OF AMERICA

O   0 9

To Ellen Steiber

WARNING!!!

Do not read this book straight through from beginning to end! These pages contain many adventures you can have while searching for the treasure of the dragons' den. From time to time as you read along, you will be asked to make a choice. Your choice may lead to success or disaster! The adventures you have will be the direct result of the decisions you make. After you make your choice, follow the instructions to see what happens to you next.

Think carefully before you make each choice, for few have ever returned from the dragons' domain. One more word of advice: beware the dragon master. He is ruthless and unpredictable!

Good luck!

It is long ago. You are in the time of knights and castles and dragons. You are a wanderer, traveling from one small medieval kingdom to another. At this moment you are in search of an adventure that will test all of your abilities and perhaps lead you to your fortune.

You are traveling through a small kingdom when you see scorched trees, burned fields, and deserted houses. The remaining local people are too terrified even to talk about what has happened, particularly with a stranger. But you know that there could be only one cause of this destruction—dragons. You also know that dragons are notorious thieves who hoard the treasure they steal. Here's your chance for some real excitement!

Turn to page 2.

That evening, while dining at a small inn, you chance to overhear two people talking at a nearby table. Treasure is being discussed, and a map is being examined. You slip quietly from your seat and move into an empty chair at their table. Taken by surprise, they look at you suspiciously.

"Now, about this treasure," you say in a low voice. "Surely you need an experienced hand to help you find it."

The two conspirators stand up and are about to bolt for the door, but you hold your hand up and they sit down again.

"Now, let's have a look at that map," you say with a grin.

"Map! What map?" one of them says. "Boke, have you seen any maps?"

"No," the other replies. He is a small, thin boy about your age. "I don't know anything about—"

"The one you have tucked into the top of your boot," you interrupt.

"Are you a king's agent?" asks the heavier one, a look of fear on his face.

"On my honor as a free wanderer, I'm not," you say.

Go on to the next page.

"Well, if you're *not* an agent, then you're going to get all three of us sent to the salt mines. The king's spies are all about. We'd better discuss this in my room. We can't all go upstairs at once—it would be too conspicuous—so we'll go one at a time. I'll go first."

"How can I trust that the two of you won't try to slip out the back of the inn, or even try to do me in upstairs?" you ask.

"Bless me! We wouldn't do that. You seem to be, if you are what you seem, the one person we're looking for," says Boke.

If you trust them and go up to the room, turn to page 10.

If you don't trust them and insist on meeting outside, turn to page 58.

You obey Zarkon's command. Suddenly there is an explosion and a bright flash of light. The bats turn in midflight and vanish back into the darkness.

"I think we're safe for the moment," Zarkon says. "Let's see if I can get a bit more light out of this stick."

Zarkon raps his staff against his arm. The end of the staff glows bright white, throwing light into the farthest reaches of the cavern. You notice Gnali over on the other side, scraping frantically at the wall. The edge of something—a door, perhaps—begins to appear under his fingers.

"I do believe you've found something," Zarkon says to him. "Stand back and I'll see what I can do."

Zarkon waves his staff back and forth at the wall. There is a cracking and splitting sound as the wall alternately expands and contracts until it finally collapses with a loud crash. A huge cloud of dust rises from the rubble. As the dust clears, an elaborately sculptured door appears, its metal gleaming in the light from Zarkon's staff.

"By my word!" exclaims Zarkon. "Will you look at that! Complete with an inscription in Dwarfish, no less. Perhaps, Gnali, you would like to translate."

The three of you look at Gnali expectantly, but he stands pale as a ghost and shaking with fear.

Turn to page 8.

"Let's hide behind the weavings," you say.

No sooner have you settled down behind them than you hear a high-pitched voice coming from one of the other rooms.

"Tarlane, where are you? I know you're here— so don't try hiding. You know I can pick up your vibrations."

"I *know* that voice," says Zarkon under his breath. "It's the sorceress Mordana. I wonder what she's doing here."

"I'll find you, Tarlane," Mordana calls, getting closer to where you are hidden. "I'm getting vibrations. I'm getting warmer."

And indeed, she is coming directly toward *you*.

"What'll we do if Mordana finds us?" you whisper to Zarkon.

"Don't worry," he says, "I think I can handle her."

Mordana is almost on top of you when there is a loud bang, like a heavy metal door being slammed shut, at the far end of the complex.

Turn to page 20.

You are looking into a luxurious chamber with deep, richly patterned rugs and ornately decorated walls. All about are large tables set with dishes and goblets of gold and silver—some encrusted with jewels. On one side of the chamber, throbbing away, is a large device made of metal and crystal. That is what you heard from below.

"This looks like a king's chamber," you whisper.

"Or that of a master thief," says Zarkon grimly.

The three of you climb up through the trapdoor and stand listening for a few moments. Then you search through the other rooms of the complex. They contain strange devices—things that you've never seen before even in your extensive travels.

"We'd better hide," says Zarkon, "I sense someone coming. Over here!" He points to a large cabinet in the corner. "It looks big enough to hold all three of us."

"No," says Virgana. She points across the room to a space piled high with large, folded pieces of cloth. "We'd be much safer behind those weavings."

"Our adventurer here has probably had a lot of experience at hiding," says Zarkon, half mockingly. "Which place do you think is best to hide in?"

If you decide to hide in the cabinet, turn to page 48.

If you decide to hide behind the weavings, turn to page 5.

8

"It . . . it's a curse directed at all dwarfs—it's t-too horrible to repeat!" Gnali stutters.

"It's the entrance to the realm of Tarlane," says Zarkon, "the dreaded dragon master himself. He's the one I've come to stop. I, for one, must go through that door."

"I'm sorry, but I can't go with you," says Gnali.

"I know," Zarkon says. "Do not feel bad. You will find another way to your people."

"I'll go with you, Zarkon," says Virgana.

"Someone should go back with Gnali and help him on his search," Zarkon says.

If you decide to go back with Gnali, turn to page 74.

If you insist on staying with Zarkon and Virgana, go on to the next page.

"I've come this far," you say. "I'm not turning back now."

"It's all right," says Gnali, "I'm quite content to try to find my way alone."

You watch Gnali disappear back down the passageway to the cave. Then you turn to the sculptured door. It pushes open easily, and you, Virgana, and Zarkon step through. You find yourselves in a corridor with walls of metal and a domed ceiling low enough for you to reach up and touch. When you do, you feel a slight tingling in your fingers.

The corridor is straight as an arrow. You walk single file for what seems like miles. Finally, you see a tiny dot of bluish light far ahead. When you reach it, you see that it is the open entrance to a small circular room. At the opposite side are three more doors, all closed. The center door has a small circle above it with an arrow drawn inside the circle. The door has no latch, but Zarkon presses a spot halfway up the door frame. Silently the door slides open, revealing a small, square room inside.

Turn to page 13.

10

Once secure in the privacy of his room, the heavy man begins his story. "My name is Reynald. A week ago I found a man lying wounded way up on Dragon Mountain. I tried to help him, but he was past help. Just before he died he gave me a map."

"What does the map show?" you ask.

Reynald unfolds a small piece of parchment. "The location of a cave high up on the side of the mountain. Whether there is treasure in the cave I don't know, but in the last minutes of his life the man mumbled something about an immense hoard of dragon treasure beneath the earth."

"Tell me how to get to this cave," you say, "and I'll give you part of any treasure I find!"

Turn to page 15.

"Zarkon," you say, "I think we should keep going into the mountain from here. Another entrance may be just as dangerous."

You wait a while until Zarkon recovers and sits up, with Virgana's help. "All right, we'll try it," he says. "Gnali, crawl in and see if the rest of us will fit."

After about fifteen minutes, Gnali returns. "The passage is tight, even for me," he reports, "but it widens out into a large cavern after about a hundred feet. It's very dark. I'll need some kind of light if I'm to go back and investigate it."

"This time we'll all go—all of us who wish to," Zarkon says, looking at Virgana.

"After you," she replies. "Age before beauty!"

"I hope you'll still have your sense of humor when this adventure is over," Zarkon mutters. With this, he disappears into the hole. The three of you follow. You get stuck a few times but make it through with nothing worse than a slightly skinned elbow and a bruised knee.

Go on to the next page.

Zarkon holds up his staff. The end of it glows bright red, like a flaming coal. Once your eyes become accustomed to the darkness, the red light is quite adequate to see by.

You are in a large cavern. Stalactites hang from the ceiling, and huge, water-carved structures, like half-melted statues, are spread across the floor.

Suddenly a horde of small, flying creatures comes sailing at you.

"Vampire bats!" Zarkon shouts. "Shut your eyes tight!"

Turn to page 4.

"I know of these rooms," says Zarkon, stroking his beard. "That one exists in our time is strange. They possess a peculiar magic. They can suddenly take you up or down. This one has all the marks of being directly controlled by Tarlane, the dragon master. We'd better avoid it if we can."

The other two doors have latches. Virgana has opened one of them. Inside, a steep circular stairway winds upward. You open the third door to find another long corridor. This one, however, has rough, jagged rock walls. Virgana comes over to look.

"This tunnel is more to my liking than that steep stairway," she says.

"The stairway is more likely to lead us to where we want to go. But I'll leave it up to you," Zarkon says, looking at you.

If you decide to follow the rough-hewn tunnel, turn to page 101.

If you decide to take the stairway, turn to page 24.

14

The three of you duck as several enormous dragons roar by the tower, narrowly missing it. The blast of wind almost blows you off the top. A number of other dragons are circling around in confusion about a half mile away. Their claws flash in the sunlight, and blasts of flame and smoke shoot out from their huge gaping mouths. One of them swoops close to the top of the tower, trying to see who now carries the dragon staff. For a moment you look into two terrible eyes.

"I hope they don't blast any flame in our direction," says Virgana. "It would roast us alive."

"As long as we have the dragon staff, I think we are safe," says Zarkon.

But then, to make matters worse, the door to the tower begins to shake. Your ears ring with the sounds of a sledgehammer being applied to the inside of the door.

"I fear that Mordana and Tarlane have already escaped our little trap," says Zarkon.

"What can we do?" you ask.

"Quick!" says Zarkon. "Hand me the dragon staff!"

Turn to page 17.

"I think I can find the cave," says Boke. "I'd like to see what's inside it myself."

"Have you forgotten the king's guard?" asks Reynald.

"There's a little-used path that we can take to get by the guard. The less they know about our comings and goings, the better."

Reynald shakes his head. "I'll stay here and wait for you to return. I don't want anything to do with dragons."

"Settled, then," you say. "Boke and I will leave at dawn."

After a few hours of sleep, you and Boke start off at daybreak. You follow a narrow, twisting street to the edge of town, and then a narrow path up into the low hills beyond.

As you near Dragon Mountain, the trail becomes steeper and steeper. Just as you are crossing a shadowy clearing, you and Boke are riveted to the ground by an unseen and powerful force.

Turn to page 26.

You hang on to the ledge by your finger tips, your feet dangling uselessly beneath you. Then, by chance, your foot catches a small outcropping of rock—just wide enough to steady you and give you a chance to catch your breath. You look up. Zarkon is above you, standing where the ledge is still firm. He is grinning and twirling a length of rope. He swings one end of it down across your back. The rope crawls around your body like a snake and fastens tightly. Then he tosses the other end to Gnali, who catches it deftly and hooks it around a large rock. Carefully, you pull yourself up, hand over hand, onto the ledge. Then you toss the end of the rope back for Zarkon and Virgana.

You are standing at the edge of the waterfall, looking into the mountain where the falls rush out of a dark tunnel.

"Now," says Zarkon briskly, "let's figure out exactly where we are. This shelf of rock obviously goes back into the tunnel. I suggest we see just how far it goes." Before anyone can object to this suggestion, Zarkon "lights up" the end of his staff and leads the way into the mountain. Slowly you follow him. Water rushes by noisily just inches below your feet.

Turn to page 25.

The door to the tower is beginning to buckle at the hinges. Zarkon waves the dragon staff in the air with one hand and his own staff with the other. Suddenly, the ugly, spined head of one of the dragons appears next to the top of the tower. The dragon's broad wings flap furiously in the air to keep it suspended there.

"I'll jump onto the dragon's head first," says Zarkon. "You two follow as quickly as you can."

The tower door is just about to give. Zarkon, then Virgana jump onto the dragon's head and cling desperately to its horns. But now that it's your turn, the dragon's head has drifted out several feet. You don't know if you can make the jump.

If you decide to try to jump to the dragon's head, turn to page 88.

If you decide to wait and take your chances with Mordana and Tarlane, turn to page 106.

Released from Zarkon's spell, you stride forward eagerly, leading the others straight up the mountain. After hours of climbing, the four of you reach the entrance to the cave.

It is a shallow cave with smooth, dark walls. All of you search the cave carefully. You find nothing inside—and no openings going deeper.

"I guess we might as well go back," Gnali says.

"Wait!" exclaims Zarkon. "I sense a hollowness beyond this part of the wall. Stand back, all of you."

In the dim light of the cave, Zarkon's eyes begin to glow. A ray of light emanates from them, striking the back wall. Slowly, a round spot on the wall begins to turn luminous red. Sparks fly from it. A hole starts to form in the rock, and then grows larger. A strong rush of air flows through the cave and into the newly formed opening.

Suddenly, Zarkon grabs his head, groans, and falls to the floor of the cave. His face is very pale. "That is the most I can do," he says. "My energy is exhausted. The underground forces here are very powerful and do not like to be disturbed. I am not sure we should use this entrance to the mountain."

If you agree with Zarkon and try to find another way into the mountain, turn to page 32.

If you try to convince Zarkon that you should explore this new opening, turn to page 11.

Zarkon interrupts your dreams of treasure to inform you that the shaft is probably a ventilating shaft.

"Maybe it'll lead to the dragons' den itself!" you say.

"It will probably lead us right into their claws," he replies. "It would be wiser to follow this river ledge to its end."

"I think we should try the shaft and go straight for the treasure," Virgana says.

If you agree with Virgana, turn to page 83.

If you agree with Zarkon, turn to page 76.

"There you are, Tarlane!" shouts Mordana. "I knew you were hiding."

"Hiding? Nonsense!" Tarlane exclaims. "I just came down from the tower."

"I see you have your dragon staff. But then you *always* do," says Mordana. "You've been up in the tower directing the dragons. How exciting! I wish you'd let *me* try it sometime."

"Forget it," Tarlane says. "It takes a lot of practice to control the dragons. You'd have them crashing into each other—or worse, crashing into the tower itself. Now, if you'll excuse me, I'm going to take a shower."

"A what?" asks Mordana.

"You know, where I get under a spray of water and wash the dirt off."

"Oh, yes, I remember now," Mordana says with a grimace. "It's one of those unhealthy, disgusting things you do."

"You're such a child of your century." Tarlane sighs.

"You dare to call me a child!"

"Just a figure of speech," says Tarlane. "And now if you'll just wait in the other room until I'm done."

Go on to the next page.

You hear the sound of a stream of water suddenly start nearby. A cloud of steam begins to rise in the room where you are hiding.

Carefully you look out from behind the weavings. You can see the vague outline of Tarlane standing in a large basin on the other side of a hanging curtain. Steaming water is pouring down on him from some spot in the ceiling. Propped up against the outside of the basin is a long, thin, metal rod—the dragon staff itself.

"Do you think you can reach Tarlane's staff without his seeing you?" Virgana whispers as she peeks out beside you.

If you try to sneak out and snatch the dragon staff, turn to page 31.

If you decide to wait, turn to page 112.

The thing you are in stops moving, and its door opens. You jump out to find yourself in a luxurious complex of rooms. The floor gleams with the luster of polished black stone. All around the room are pieces of furniture made of richly grained woods and other objects of silver and gold. Some are studded with diamonds and other gems.

As you wander about, you find more rooms furnished with more riches. In one of them you discover a display case made of shimmering crystal and framed with gold. Resting inside it is a gleaming sword with a polished steel blade and a handle of inlaid ivory.

Something about the sword—beyond its beauty and obvious value—fascinates you. Your palms itch to hold it. But would it be wise to take it from its case? Could it be a trap of some sort, put there to tempt the unwary?

If you decide to take the sword,
turn to page 34.

If you decide to leave well enough alone,
turn to page 108.

There are just too many guards around. You'll have to try to escape later. The guards untie Boke and his friend and then lead the three of you at swordpoint up to the castle.

"Take them to the dungeon," an officer of the guard orders.

Alone, you are shoved inside a grim, barren stone cell. Its heavy iron door slams shut, and you can hear the guards marching away.

Turn to page 28.

You agree with Zarkon that the circular stairway is the best way to go. But after a half hour of climbing steadily upward, you are not so sure that you made the right choice. You are tired—and dizzy from going around in circles—but you keep climbing.

"Stop a moment," says Zarkon. "I think I hear something."

The three of you listen. Far above, you hear a throbbing sound.

"What is it?" Virgana whispers.

"It could be a dragon breathing," you suggest.

"Perhaps," says Zarkon. "More likely some evil device of the dragon master."

Turn to page 30.

Soon you hear another sound over the water, a low whistle. Then, with the help of the light from Zarkon's staff, you see where the whistle is coming from. Halfway up the wall is a perfect round hole about Gnali's height in diameter. Air is being sucked inside it from the river tunnel. Gnali, holding Zarkon's staff, stands on your shoulders to examine it. "The shaft goes down at a slight angle," he reports, "and it's very smooth inside. I smell something burnt, like sulfur. It's the smell of dragons."

"And where there are dragons, there is treasure!" you say.

Turn to page 19.

A burst of hearty laughter comes from the trees as a tall, bearded figure wearing a long, elaborately patterned cloak steps into the clearing. He carries a long carved staff.

"The wizard—Zarkon!" exclaims Boke.

"So you would dare to enter the cave in the mountain," Zarkon says. "You would go down to the dragons' den itself, I'll wager—for treasure. Don't look so surprised. I've just been reading your minds. Nothing much to that."

Zarkon laughs again. "And you, Virgana—disguised as a boy, no less," he says pointing his staff at Boke. With that, Boke's hat flies off, revealing a full head of beautiful blonde hair which, coming undone, falls to her shoulders.

"You're an old meddler, Zarkon," says Boke— whom you realize you must now call Virgana. "Stay out of this. We mean to find our fortunes and return."

Zarkon frowns. "Watch your tongue, young lady. I could easily change you into a tadpole. Luckily, I like your spirit." Then he turns to you. "And you, wanderer, are the one I have waited for. Your guidance will be invaluable to me. Let me introduce you to a friend."

Turn to page 33.

Early the next morning, the guards come back for you. You are led up to the king's audience chamber. Boke and his friend are also there.

"What is the charge against these three?" demands the king.

"Conspiracy to hunt for treasure in secret, Your Highness," states one of the guards.

"Treasure!" exclaims the king. "What treasure?"

"This is all a misunderstanding," says Boke. "We heard a rumor that there might be treasure in a cave up on the mountain. We were on our way to the castle to report it to the authorities when we were stopped by your guard."

"A cave—on the mountain!" exclaims the king. "There's only one mountain around here, and that's Dragon Mountain."

"Your Highness, we only—" you start.

"We mustn't do anything—I repeat, anything—to rouse the dragons inside the mountain," the king says. "If we do, they will swoop down and devastate my kingdom again. We haven't finished rebuilding from their last attack."

Go on to the next page.

"Maybe the dragons can be stopped," you say.

"Bosh!" snaps the king. "My wizard, Zarkon, has been trying to stop them for years—and without success. Now if you're all so anxious to go into the mountain, a term in the salt mines should satisfy your curiosity. Take them away!"

"You can't do that!" shouts Boke.

"And why can't I?" demands the king.

"Because of this," Boke says, pulling off his cap.

Turn to page 38.

"Just who or what is this dragon master?" you ask.

"There are many legends about him," answers Zarkon. "Some say that he has traveled back into our time from the future."

"How can anyone come *back* from the future?" asks Virgana.

"There are things stranger than you imagine," Zarkon says with a chuckle. "In fact, there are things stranger than you *can* imagine. Wizards like myself know something of this."

"Is the dragon master a wizard?" you ask.

"I don't think so," Zarkon replies thoughtfully. "He is something different—what, even I am not sure. I do know that with his dragons, he has spread death and destruction across the kingdoms. He must be stopped."

"Well, dragon master or not," says Virgana, "let's go up and find out what's there."

The three of you continue cautiously up the stairs until you reach a trapdoor closed above you. You listen quietly for a while. Then slowly you push the trapdoor open an inch or so. What you see makes you gasp.

Turn to page 7.

As quietly as you can, you sneak out into the steam-filled room and, on your hands and knees, crawl to the staff. You grab it and sneak back to the pile of weavings.

"While Tarlane is still preoccupied," whispers Zarkon, "I'm going to confront Mordana. You must not let go of the dragon staff, and don't come out until I tell you. I have a plan."

Turn to page 37.

"All right, Zarkon," you say. "If you know another way into the mountain, I'm willing to try it."

You, Virgana, and Gnali follow Zarkon outside the cave. "There is a path that leads around the mountain and will take us to where Gnali was swept away," he says.

The sun is now high in the sky. You walk single file along the narrow path, which does not go upward but leads gradually down until you are back among the small gnarled trees at the upper reaches of the forest. You become aware of a roaring sound coming from somewhere ahead of you. The roar gets louder and louder. At the top of a high hill you step out into a clearing and look at the side of the mountain; a waterfall pours out of a sheer cliff and plunges hundreds of feet down to a lake below.

"You really think this way will be safer?" you ask, looking up toward the falls.

"You may have a point there," Zarkon replies, "but we're here, and there's a path that winds up above the falls. We could rope down to the entrance to the mountain from above. I happen to have a stout length of rope in my cloak.

"There is also a narrow ledge in the rock face on the other side of the cliff that leads to the opening. I'm sure our adventurer here will know which way is best."

If you decide to follow the narrow ledge across the rock, turn to page 46.

If you decide to rope down from above, turn to page 89.

The small figure of a dwarf child jumps into view.

"This is Gnali, one of the few dwarfs ever to have left Dragon Mountain," Zarkon continues. "Three years ago, he fell into an underground stream that carried him out of the mountain over a waterfall. Miraculously unharmed, he was found on the bank of the lake below by a woodcutter. Since then, Gnali has been raised by the woodcutter's family. Now he wants to go back into the mountain and return to his own family. Since my mission takes me to Dragon Mountain, I have promised to help him find his home. If you and Virgana will join us, perhaps we can help each other."

"We don't have much choice," Virgana whispers.

"Exactly," agrees Zarkon. "Now if memory serves me, we can take this path straight up the mountain—a rough climb, but it's the fastest way. Or we can take the other path, which follows a longer winding route. That way will leave us in better shape to explore the cave once we get there. We'll let our young adventurer decide."

If you decide to go straight up the mountain, turn to page 18.

If you decide to take a winding route, turn to page 86.

You slide open the top of the case and reach for the sword. The handle fits perfectly in your hand. As you lift the sword out of the case, a strange force seems to run up through your arm. You slash the blade through the air to get the feel of it, and the sword leaves a glow in the air where it passed.

You are about to try it again when you hear voices coming. You duck behind a heavy, elaborately carved standing screen. Just in time! Through a crack in the screen you see a man and a woman come into the room.

"But, Tarlane," the woman says, "you said you'd show me how you control the dragons in exchange for some of *my* secrets. Remember, with my occult powers and your dragons, we could control the world."

"Right, Mordana," Tarlane says, "but now I'm preparing an important mission. On top of that, some of the dragons are acting up—why, I'm not sure."

"Well, dragons will be dragons, I always say," says Mordana.

Tarlane ushers her to the door. She goes out and he closes it behind her. Then he spins on his heels and takes a small metal object from his jacket. He walks over and stands in front of the screen you are hiding behind. The metal object in his hand is pointed at you!

"All right, whoever you are, come out from behind that screen," he orders.

Turn to page 40.

Zarkon disappears into the other room. You can just barely hear him talking with Mordana. Fortunately, Tarlane has started singing to himself. You hope he can't hear them at all.

"Zarkon, what are you doing here!" Mordana exclaims.

"Just passing through," Zarkon replies. "And you—you've teamed up with this crazy dragon master?"

"Hardly," says Mordana, indignantly, "but I have use of him."

"Ah, the dragon staff is what you're after," says Zarkon.

"Perhaps."

"Did you say something?" Tarlane calls out over the sound of the flowing water.

"Just talking to myself," Mordana calls back. Then she says softly to Zarkon, "You'd better get out of here fast."

"All right, Mordana," says Zarkon. "I'm going back through the trapdoor. See you again some-time."

Suddenly Tarlane stops singing and turns off the water. All is quiet for a moment. Tarlane steps out of the basin, dripping wet. He reaches over and grabs for one of the pieces of cloth. Unfortunately, he grabs *you* by the hair.

Turn to page 39.

Long blonde shoulder-length hair tumbles free. "I'm a girl and my name is Virgana," says the small, thin youth you know as Boke.

"On my word!" exclaims the king. "No, the salt mines wouldn't do for a girl. Frail things they are—wouldn't last an hour in the mines."

"I resent that!" exclaims Virgana. "Women can do any job that a man can."

"Then why, in heaven's name, can't you work in the mines?" asks the king.

"Because it's not right for the times," says a heavy, low voice coming from a side door.

"My wizard, Zarkon!" exclaims the king. "I'm glad you're here. What am I to do about all this?"

"Well, for this young lady," says Zarkon, "how about a period of being a serving maid in the castle? As for the other two, I'd give them a choice between a short term in the mines or total banishment from the kingdom."

The mines can't be too far from the cave with the treasure, you think. If you can escape, then . . .

"I'll take banishment," says Virgana's friend.

If you choose a short term in the mines, turn to page 42.

If you choose total banishment from the kingdom, turn to page 109.

"Ugh!" cries Tarlane, releasing your hair. "I've got to send these towels to the laundry."

He takes one of the weavings, dries himself off and puts on a robe. Then, just as you feared, Tarlane begins to search for his staff. "All right, Mordana, where did you put it?"

"What do you mean?" Mordana asks indignantly.

"Listen, Mordana, I left my dragon staff leaning against the tub while I took a shower, and now it's gone. Since you're the only one here besides me, I assume that you took it."

"But I'm not the only one here, or at least I wasn't until a few moments ago," Mordana says. "Zarkon the wizard just popped through here."

"Where did he go?" shouts Tarlane in a panic.

"Promise to show me how to use the dragon staff and I'll tell you," Mordana says.

"All right, all right!" Tarlane exclaims. "Just tell me!"

"He went through that trapdoor over there," Mordana says.

"Good!" Tarlane exclaims. "We'll head him off easily. Quick, into the elevator!"

Turn to page 59.

Using all your might, you shove the heavy screen toward Tarlane. He leaps aside, but the top of the falling screen catches his foot, and he tumbles to the floor. He tries to point the metal object in your direction again, but a slash from the sword knocks the weapon from his hand. It sails across the floor and under a chair. Quickly, Tarlane is on his feet. Seemingly from nowhere, he grabs a long metal staff and swings it at you. That's his mistake. You catch the staff with the sword and cut it in two. A surge of the sword's own force shoots back through the blade and into your body. You are momentarily frozen to the spot. Tarlane is not so lucky. The part of the staff he still holds explodes in his hands, knocking him back into another room.

Turn to page 53.

"No punishment could be worse than banishment from your fair kingdom," you answer the king, even though you have to bite your tongue to keep from laughing.

"Nobly spoken," says the king. "Perhaps we can just send you to the mines as an *observer*— for a short period. That should be enough to scare you back into the straight and narrow. Now begone, before I change my mind."

Early the next day, you are put into a wagon with a group of prisoners being sent to the mines. The horse-drawn wagons move slowly, their heavy wooden wheels jouncing over the rocky road. You see wagons coming back the other way loaded with blocks of raw salt. Finally, just after sundown, you reach the mines.

The mining goes on day and night by torchlight. You are assigned the job of carrying water to the prisoners while they dig. As water bearer, you are allowed to roam freely through the mine. You carry a large earthenware jug, and with a long ladle, you pour water into the small clay cups that each miner carries on a cord.

Go on to the next page.

For several weeks, you work and sleep in the mines. Your term as an observer is about up. On your last day, you are deep inside the mazelike complex of tunnels that make up the mine when you hear the sound of running feet and cries of panic. The guards come dashing by, followed by a number of prisoners. One of the last prisoners spots you standing by one of the big, square pillars of salt that support the ceilings of the underground passageways.

"Run for it!" he shouts. "The king's men will be sealing off this part of the mine in a few minutes!"

Turn to page 47.

"I think I'll keep going up the mountain," you say.

"I'm with you," says Virgana.

Gnali also nods yes.

"Thanks for bringing us this far," you tell the troopers as you step over the dragon line. You turn to wave goodbye as they ride off down the slope.

"Looks as if we're on our own," you say.

"Looks like it," Virgana agrees. "And even with the map," she says, taking it out of her boot, "I still can't tell where that cave is."

"Cave or no cave," you say, "I think we're on to something. You see that tower up there? That could mark an entrance into the mountain."

"It also appears to mark the top of the mountain," says Gnali. You ignore his remark and climb toward the tower.

You are almost there when you notice a number of large black shapes in the southern sky. They're closing fast.

"I don't like the looks of those things," you say. "Let's make a dash for the tower. There may be a door at its base."

Turn to page 110.

"Let's try the tower," you say. "The door to it must be down this way."

It is. Virgana shakes her head in disbelief as the three of you start up the tower stairs.

"We must find a way to destroy the dragon staff," Zarkon says.

"Can't we just smash it or throw it off the top of the tower?" you ask.

"I don't think so," he answers. "It might just release the dragons and cause devastation in a new, uncontrolled way."

Soon you reach the top of the tower. You close the door to the platform and lock it from the outside.

"No wonder Tarlane can direct his dragons from up here," Zarkon says. "We can see half a dozen kingdoms down there."

The dragon staff in your hand begins to beep. There's a row of small bumps along one side of the staff. They push in when you press on them and pop out again when you release the pressure. Far on the horizon, a row of black spots bobs in the sky.

"I don't understand this," you say to Zarkon. "When I press the top bumps on the staff, the black dots disappear. When I press the bottom bumps, the dots come back."

"Those black dots must be dragons many leagues away," Zarkon says. "You are doing something with them or to them. This bodes ill, I fear. I must try to contact the eagles before it is too late."

Turn to page 52.

"Now that we've got the dragon staff, what should we do?" you ask.

"Find the stairs to Tarlane's tower," Zarkon replies. "If we reach the top I can try to call the eagles to rescue us."

"Eagles!" exclaims Virgana. "You must be joking. I think we should search for an exit down here." She turns to you and asks, "What do you think?"

If you decide to try to find the tower stairs, turn to page 44.

If you decide to look for an exit here, turn to page 78.

"Let's give the ledge a try," you say. "If it's really wide enough to keep our footing, it seems like the easiest way."

You follow Zarkon down a winding path to the edge of the lake and then along its shore to the other side of the cliff. Then Zarkon leads you up again along a steeper path. Before long the path turns into a vertical series of rock holds. Finally, you reach a point across from the opening to the falls. From there you can see the narrow ledge that Zarkon was talking about. It is *very* narrow— a few inches wide—tracing a thin line across the cliff.

"Let me go first," says Gnali. "Not only am I smaller and lighter than the rest of you, but I want to be the first to go into the tunnel that leads back to my home."

"All right, Gnali," Zarkon says. "But be careful!"

Turn to page 50.

Instantly you remember what you were told a few days earlier. If the miners accidentally break through into a dragon run—one of the many large tunnels carved by the dragons under the mountain—then that part of the mine is sealed off.

You turn to follow the prisoner who warned you—then stop as you realize this accident might be a great way of getting into dragon territory. The dragon run may lead directly to a hoard of treasure! You can worry about how to get out of the mountain once you grab some of it. On the other hand, if you encounter a dragon, one puff of its breath can burn you to a cinder.

You have to decide quickly.

If you try to run back before they seal off this part of the mine, turn to page 99.

If you decide to go forward and explore the dragon territory, turn to page 65.

"That's a strange-looking cabinet," you say. "Still, it's large enough to hold the three of us easily."

The three of you quickly climb inside. As you close the door behind you, there is a click and then a whirring sound. You didn't expect *that*. Suddenly, you are whirled around, spinning faster and faster. You struggle to get the door open. But it is no use—and you are rapidly losing consciousness.

Turn to page 56.

"There is something about this device that I definitely don't like," you say. "Let's go back to the forest cover as fast as we can."

"I'll second that," says one of the troopers. "Jump on and let's get out of here."

Fortunately, going downhill is faster for the horses. But it still seems like an eternity before you reach the woods. Something in the back of your mind is shouting danger!

When you get to the woods, the troopers hide their horses among the trees to rest. Then you go back to the edge of the woods and look up the slope. Far up on top of the mountain you see black shapes circling. They could be birds. But birds flying at such a great distance would barely be visible from where you are. You know the circling shapes are something much larger—dragons!

"I don't know about you," you say to Virgana and Gnali, "but I'm going deeper into the forest for a while. I have to decide if I really want that dragon treasure as much as I thought I did."

The End

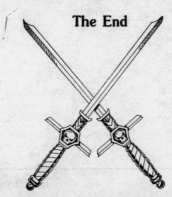

50

The rest of you watch as Gnali inches his way, step by step, toward the falls. Finally, he disappears around a corner and vanishes into the opening. Moments later, his head reappears.

"It's all right," he shouts.

You go next, pressing yourself as tightly as you can against the rock. Carefully you work your way along the ledge. You don't dare look down. You're afraid that you might get dizzy and fall off.

You've almost reached the opening in the cliff where Gnali waits. Suddenly, the rock ledge starts to crumble under your feet! You begin to slide down the face of the cliff. Frantically you reach out for any possible handhold. Finally your fingers grab on to what is left of the ledge.

Turn to page 16.

52

But before Zarkon can do anything, you notice that the dots have grown into definite shapes and are getting larger by the second. The dragons are heading back to the tower! Frantically you press all the small bumps on the staff. But it doesn't turn the formation of dragons back. Soon they are immense shapes blocking out the sun and hurtling straight at you!

Turn to page 14.

With bloody hands, Tarlane crawls toward a cabinet in the corner. You assume he wants to get some new weapon. Free now of the paralyzing force, you run to stop him. You grab him just as he is crawling into the cabinet. With a strength you didn't suspect he had, Tarlane pulls you inside with him. The doors of the cabinet slam shut.

A flash like a bolt of lightning stuns you. Everything spins around—faster and faster. Then, as suddenly as it began, the spinning stops.

Turn to page 116.

Suddenly you come out of the tunnel onto a narrow slab of rock that juts out over a vast, circular pit. You almost stumble into it, but you catch yourself in time and warn Virgana and Zarkon who are behind you. The three of you huddle on the narrow ledge, bracing yourselves against the wall. Seconds later, the fire lizard charges out of the tunnel. Unable to stop itself, it sails out over the pit. You see its evil claws flash in the air—its legs flailing in desperation as it arcs into the depths below. A piercing wail echoes about the circular pit as the fire lizard disappears into the void. The sound of its scream becomes fainter and fainter, trailing out to complete silence. You strain to hear the fire lizard hit bottom. You never do.

Then you hear another roar from the tunnel behind you. Another fire lizard is racing toward you! Quickly all three of you squeeze back against the wall.

But this fire lizard manages to stop just in time to keep from falling over the edge. It sits there with blazing eyes, watching you.

How long can you balance on the narrow ledge—trapped between the bottomless pit and the fire lizard?

Not long!

The End

When you wake up, the whirling has stopped. The door clicks open again. You shake your head to get rid of the grogginess in it. Aside from feeling dizzy, the three of you are all right. You brace yourselves for a confrontation with whoever might be outside the cabinet. But when you peek out, no one is there. Instead, the room that the cabinet was in when you entered it has been replaced by a much larger room. One that is filled with the same kind of devices that were in the old room—but there are so many more of them! On the other side of the room, a long, high window looks out over a broad valley ringed by tall mountains. A door next to the window leads outside. The three of you go out. The view is breathtaking. In the distance are many strange-looking buildings and structures.

"By some magic that I don't understand," says Zarkon, "we've been transported in time—into the future, from the looks of it."

As he says this, you hear a heavy droning overhead in the sky.

"If we've traveled in time," you say, "the dragons have followed us. Look up there!"

Turn to page 79.

Below you is an immense cavern, while above is a large, fire-blackened shaft which must go all the way to the surface of the mountain. The dusty column of light that shines down through the shaft strikes the backs of two huge dragons sleeping on top of an enormous mound of treasure! The dragons' deep rumbling snores echo off the rocks. There can be no doubt. You have found the dragons' den.

"Look at that," you say, awed. "I didn't know there was that much treasure in the whole world!"

"If we could only get down there, it would be all ours," says Virgana.

"I'm for climbing back up this shaft," Gnali says.

Zarkon takes you aside. "Virgana is clearly consumed with greed, and Gnali seems terrified by the dragons. Your mind is still clear, so *you* must decide."

If you decide to try to get back up the ventilator shaft, turn to page 80.

If you decide to try to get into the dragons' den, turn to page 73.

"I think it would be better if we met outside," you say. "I have a certain distrust of upstairs rooms."

"Very well," says Boke. "We can meet at the end of the lane in an hour. But watch out for the king's patrols. They can be nasty."

Boke and his friend leave by the back door of the inn.

When almost an hour has gone by, you casually pay for your meal and ease out the front door. The lane is dark. Every so often a sliver of moon appears from behind a cloud and casts a pale light on the town. But your eyes are used to seeing in the dark. Far up the lane, you see Boke and his friend standing together by a post. You stride toward them in the darkness. You've almost reached them when you realize that there is something very wrong. Then you see that Boke and his friend are not just standing by the post— they're tied to it!

"Run for it!" Boke shouts to you. "It's a trap!"

Turn to page 71.

"Into the what?" asks Mordana.

"Never mind, just get in," Tarlane says, pushing her into a small room with a circled arrow over the door like the one you saw down below. The door closes, and the arrow starts to move.

Suddenly, Zarkon is back up through the trapdoor. "They fell for it!" he cries. "Come on out." Then he points his staff at the moving arrow. An explosion blasts away part of the wall above the door. "That should hold them awhile," he says. "They're trapped in the shaft."

Turn to page 45.

It's dark inside. The three of you go in, and Zarkon lights his staff so that you can see.

"I think we made a mistake," he says as he looks around. "Let's try another way."

You go back to the heavy door. But while you were looking around, it had quietly closed and locked itself. The inside of the door is featureless, shiny metal. There's no latch on your side.

"Looks like we're stuck with this way," you say.

Turn to page 72.

"As if I could forget," Valerian groans. "All right, we'll bend the rules a bit."

Valerian divides up the troop. Five of the guard, including himself, will return with Zarkon. The other five will escort you up the mountain.

"I will rejoin you soon—I hope!" Zarkon calls as he jumps on the back of Valerian's horse. You watch as they gallop back down the mountain. Then you, Virgana, and Gnali each climb up behind a horseman and continue on up the mountain.

Turn to page 66.

You have only seconds to act. Frantically you feel along the side of the tunnel. Luckily you stumble into a deep recess in the wall. And none too soon! A dragon roars by a second later.

You lie there panting for breath—trying to pull yourself together. As you do, you feel a steady stream of cool air from somewhere above you. You stand up and feel along the wall. Above you, your searching fingers find a round hole. It might be a connecting passage to another tunnel.

You've had enough of *this* particular dragon run for the moment! Using the rough stones of the alcove wall, you climb up to the opening and slide inside. Unfortunately, the passageway isn't large enough to stand up in, and you have to walk bent over in a low crouch.

You go on and on like this, stopping frequently to rest. Finally, you hear something up ahead. The sound of rushing water! Soon the bottom of the passageway becomes damp, then gradually fills with water until it is waist high. You can feel the entrances to other tunnels to the sides, but you keep going straight along the one you are in.

Go on to the next page.

The tunnel ends suddenly at the edge of a broad river flowing rapidly through a high cavern. The phosphorescence of the rushing water creates a dim glow—just enough for you to see to the other side. There you see a fairly continuous ledge just above the water line. The current seems strong, but you may be able to reach the ledge—even if you get carried some distance downstream before you reach it.

If you try to swim across the river to the ledge on the other side, turn to page 98.

If you decide to go back and try one of the branching tunnels, turn to page 115.

The reason you chose the salt mines in the first place was to find dragon treasure. This may be your only chance!

Carefully you rest the water jug against a pillar. You take one of the torches from its holder in the wall and walk cautiously down the same passageway the miners had fled. A few minutes later you come to the spot where the diggers broke through into the dragon run. Part of the wall has collapsed. You stand before a gaping hole; pushing your torch through, you take a look.

The tunnel is roughly circular with jagged walls. The floor, though, is relatively smooth. You climb through the hole into the tunnel.

You walk briskly for what seems like hours. The sound of your footsteps echoes through the silent tunnel.

Without knowing why, you stop and listen. Suddenly, your torch goes out. You are left in total darkness. Far off you hear a faint, roaring sound. You walk a little farther, guided by the feel of the tunnel floor.

You stop again. The roaring is louder this time. Then far off down the tunnel you see two small spots of red racing toward you. You feel a little sick as you realize that they are probably the blazing eyes of a dragon—charging down the tunnel straight at you!

Turn to page 62.

It is late afternoon when you see a tower at the top of the mountain. At the same time, the horses stop before a strange structure on the ground—a low fence of thick metal threads running in both directions as far as you can see. You dismount, touch one of the threads, and instantly jerk your arm back in pain. The fence is burning hot.

You try to step over the metal threads, but one of the troopers reaches over and grabs you. "This is the dragon line," he says. "The king has forbidden us to cross it. The dragons will know if we do."

"How?" you ask. "The dragons are supposed to be under the mountain—miles away."

"I know not what evil magic is at play here," replies the trooper, "but I would not tempt fate. You may go on at your own risk, but my men and I are returning to the castle—no matter what Zarkon asked us to do. I would advise that you do the same."

If you take the trooper's advice and return down the mountain, turn to page 49.

If you decide to cross the dragon line and continue up the mountain, turn to page 43.

"Who are—" you start.

"Just a moment," says the dwarf. "Another is coming."

A few seconds later, Zarkon comes into view, his staff glowing in the dim light.

"Zarkon!" you exclaim. "I remember you—you're the king's wizard. But what are you doing here?"

"For one thing," Zarkon says, "I'm helping my friend Gnali here to get safely back to his people under this mountain. And you, I see, are still in search of treasure."

"That's right," you say.

"Then you have a choice," says Zarkon. "You can go with Gnali and me to search for the land of the dwarfs, and then let me help you find your treasure. Or you can follow that tunnel that starts up there on the wall—it leads directly to the dragons' den. But I must warn you that the second choice is a very dangerous one."

If you decide to go to the land of the dwarfs, turn to page 97.

If you decide to take the tunnel that leads to the dragons' den, turn to page 81.

You rush at the guard with the lantern. He is not prepared for your attack and falls backward to the ground, stunned. The lantern flies out of his hand and crashes into darkness on the road.

You run with all your might down the street toward a bridge. An object whizzes by your head. Then another. Arrows! The guards have archers posted on the town wall. But you are fast and the night is dark. You are halfway across the bridge when, suddenly, the moon reappears. An arrow strikes you in the back—then another and another.

You topple lifeless into the moat.

The End

You turn and dash down the lane. Your way is suddenly blocked by dim shadows. Even though you can't see them clearly, your experience tells you that they are the king's guard. And you sense that their swords are drawn and pointed at you.

You stand there for a moment, trying to decide what to do. One of the guards opens a lantern. Its beam falls on your face.

"That's the one," a woman's voice says. You remember that voice. It belongs to the serving girl who waited on you at the inn. She must have overheard you talking about the treasure map!

"Good work, Molly," says the guard holding the lantern. You hear the faint clink of coins being passed. On hearing that, you realize the guard must have put his sword back in his belt in order to give Molly the money. And he is the only one standing between you and a side street!

If you try to rush by the guard and escape down the side street, turn to page 68.

If you decide that you are outnumbered and you'd better wait, turn to page 23.

Zarkon shakes his head. "I fear we are inside the base of Tarlane's tower." He opens a door on the other side of the room. "See! Here is a stairway."

"Let's go up," says Virgana. "Maybe there's a way to get down on the outside of the tower."

"It's possible," says Zarkon. "I have a plan."

The three of you climb up the stairway. At the top you come out onto a platform with a low railing. The view is incredible. But when you look down the outside of the tower, you see that the sides are of sheer, almost polished, stone.

Then, far in the distance and close to the horizon, you see black spots dancing in the sky.

"Do you see those?" asks Virgana. "They might be dragons."

"They are," says Zarkon, "and they could return at any moment. That huge burned scar on the mountain over there is their dragon hole."

Turn to page 114.

"The dragons' den it is," says Zarkon. "First, this row of bars was almost knocked loose when we hit it. We're lucky that we didn't all go flying into the dragons' den. A few good kicks will knock the grating free. Let's all kick together now. One, two, three—kick!"

The grating breaks loose. It arcs downward, and bounces off the ugly horned head of one of the dragons! The dragon raises its head slightly and looks around with baleful eyes. Then it snorts a few jets of flame and finally falls back to snoring.

"That gives me an idea," says Zarkon. "Everyone be quiet while I concentrate."

Zarkon's eyes begin to glow. A faint beam of light starts to form between his eyes and the tail of one of the dragons. After a while, the dragon's tail begins to glow red. A thin wisp of smoke rises from it. Suddenly, the dragon awakes and leaps up with a roar that shakes the whole cavern, breaking stones loose from the ceiling and almost knocking the four of you down into the cavern. The other dragon raises its head—its eyes still glazed with sleep. Then the first dragon, using its tail, bats the other one in the head with such force that it causes another shower of rocks from the ceiling.

Turn to page 87.

"I guess I should go with Gnali," you say. "He'll need help if he is going to find his people."

"Good luck to you both," says Zarkon with one of his rare smiles.

You follow Gnali back into the low, narrow passageway leading to the cave. Gnali, being so small, is quickly ahead of you. Again you have trouble squeezing through. Suddenly, you come to a point where the passageway divides right and left. You don't remember passing this fork on the way in, but feeling your way along in the darkness, you could easily have missed it.

Then from far off down one of the passageways, you hear Gnali's voice calling. You crawl in that direction. And come to another fork! You strain to catch the sound of Gnali's voice again. You hear a muffled sound to the right. If it's Gnali, he's much farther off this time, but you follow the sound anyway.

Soon you find yourself back at the same fork. You try a different direction. It doesn't help. No matter which way you go, you return to the same fork. You are going around in circles!

You'll be going around in circles for a long, long time.

The End

Something behind you makes you turn. An apelike creature with long, jagged teeth is charging at you. There is nowhere to go except over the narrow stone arch. You decide to risk it, and hope that the soles of your shoes will protect your feet long enough for you to get to the other side. You try a quick dash over the hot span. But the heat and suffocating fumes are too much for you. You collapse at the center of the stone arch. The creature pounces on you—but you are already finished.

The End

"As long as there *is* a path along the river, I think we should follow it," you say.

You hike deep into the mountain. As the ledge curves, you come across a low tunnel. Gnali is almost overcome with joy and excitement. It's a dwarf hole! You're happy for Gnali, but you're not overjoyed at having to walk half bent over in a tunnel meant for dwarfs. By the time you reach the main dwarf town, a high-walled cavern filled with hundreds of circular dwarf houses, you are so stiff that it takes half an hour before you can stand up straight again.

You, Virgana, and Zarkon have helped Gnali return to his family. There is rejoicing throughout the underground lands of the dwarfs. They hold a giant feast in your honor. The dwarfs' banquet hall is decorated with tapestries woven with gold threads that sparkle in the bright torchlight. You are served mushrooms, fish from the underground lakes, and other delicacies whose source you do not care to know.

Go on to the next page.

The next morning you and your companions are loaded with sacks of uncut gems and gold nuggets. Then the dwarfs lead you up through the mountain to an exit known only to them.

You and Virgana are so excited you can't stop talking about your good fortune. You didn't find the dragon treasure, but you are now wealthy beyond your dreams.

The End

"Virgana's right. There must be an exit some-where around here," you say.

The three of you quickly search every room and corridor in the complex. Finally, Virgana finds the door to a tunnel at the far end of a cor-ridor.

You and Zarkon follow her in to investigate. Suddenly the tunnel fills with a thick green gas.

"It's a trap!" you scream, helplessly gasping for air. But before you know it you become confused and disoriented. The gas is affecting your mind. Somehow you know what you are seeing is all an illusion, but still you can't stop the rush of horrible images . . . hundreds of monsters circling your feet, then slowly climbing up your legs. You shake them off. But they return as skinless lizards that cling to your neck, their fangs glistening.

This illusion will continue for a long, long time.

The End

Hundreds of black, crosslike shapes fill the sky.

"What is happening?" asks Virgana. "Could those be dragons dropping their eggs?"

"Run!" you shout in a panic. You race for the cover of a nearby grove of trees.

Suddenly there are tremendous explosions all around you. One of them destroys the inside of the building you just came out of. Zarkon pulls you and Virgana to the ground just in time to save you from being hit by pieces of the windows flying through the air.

"I have a horrible feeling," says Zarkon, "that we have just traveled forward in time to a period that makes the time we come from seem very peaceful. And I'm afraid our chances of returning to *our* time were just blown up."

The End

"There's got to be a safer way," you tell Virgana. "I think we should go back up the ventilation shaft and try to find another entrance to the dragons' den."

"It's going to be hard—and risky—to get back up that shaft," says Zarkon, "but let's give it a try."

Zarkon tosses his rope into the shaft. The rope crawls upward as if it were alive, then attaches itself somewhere far up the tunnel.

"It can't have much to grasp on to up there," says Zarkon, "but it seems to be holding."

Zarkon goes first, pulling himself gradually upward with the rope. You go next, followed by Virgana and Gnali.

Suddenly, you hear Zarkon cursing above you. Then he comes flying down on top of you, the rope loose in his hands. As both of you go sliding down you pick up Virgana and Gnali. All of you crash into the row of bars again. This time the grating breaks loose and goes flying—the four of you with it—into the dragons' den.

The dragons wake up with a roar, hungry for an early morning snack—you!

The End

You climb up into the tunnel leading to the dragons' den. The inside of the tunnel is so smooth that you can easily push yourself along. You're confident that the treasure will soon be yours.

As the tunnel slants downward it becomes steeper and steeper. You can't hold yourself back anymore. You are sliding out of control! Just when you think that nothing can save you, the tunnel gradually levels out, and you tumble to a stop behind a row of vertical bars. You are high above the dragons' den. And you are in big trouble! There is no way through the bars, and the tunnel is too steep and too slippery to climb back up.

Eventually, Zarkon may find a way to rescue you, but for now you will stay where you are—trapped!

The End

You struggle through the hole in the ventilating shaft, Virgana close behind. You slide down the inside of the shaft, pressing your hands against the sides to keep from going too fast. Zarkon, Virgana, and Gnali follow.

You don't notice it at first, but the tunnel gets gradually steeper as you go along. You have difficulty keeping yourself from going too fast. Soon you realize that you couldn't stop even if you wanted to. From the cries behind you, you know that the others are having the same trouble.

At last the tunnel levels out, but before you can slow yourself down, you wham into a row of bars. A few seconds later, Zarkon, Virgana, and Gnali tumble into you. It takes a moment to untangle yourselves. When you do, you look down through the bars. You can hardly believe what you see!

Turn to page 57.

Zarkon's rope almost reaches to the floor of the cavern—but not quite. You have to drop the last ten feet. Fortunately, a great mound of pearls below breaks your fall. Nearby, diamonds, amethysts, and rubies are piled high. You can't believe your eyes. You've never seen such treasure. Excitedly, you and Virgana start stuffing your pockets with jewels. Gnali and Zarkon, both oblivious to the treasure, are already looking for ways out of the cavern.

"I remember being told," says Gnali, "that there is a secret dwarf peephole high up on the side of the dragons' den. But I don't think it is large enough for even a dwarf to crawl through."

"The main dragon door seems to be over there," says Zarkon, pointing. "It probably leads to the nursery where the dragon eggs are hatched. And baby dragons are especially dangerous."

"Look," says Gnali. "On the wall up there—a small balcony. I think we could climb up there. It doesn't look that high."

Zarkon looks doubtful. "It could be the dragon master's observation post, and if he's there, it could also be our end. Our choice is between the dragon door and the dragon master's balcony. What do you think?" he asks, looking at you.

If you decide to go through the dragon door, turn to page 103.

If you decide to climb up to the balcony, turn to page 92.

"I don't see any use in wearing ourselves out," you say as you start up the winding path.

The four of you climb easily and steadily higher until the woods start to thin out. Ahead, through the last of the trees, you see a broad alpine meadow sloping up toward the top of the mountain high above you.

You are halfway across the meadow when you hear noises behind you. Turning, you see a large group of soldiers on horseback charging toward you.

Turn to page 94.

"The dragon with the burnt tail thinks the other one did it," whispers Virgana.

The two dragons leap up, snarling, and go at each other with horrible roars.

Still fighting, the two dragons fly up through the dragon hole at the top of the cavern. The den is plunged into darkness for a few seconds; then the light returns. Zarkon has already lowered his rope as far down as it will go into the dragons' den.

"Quickly! Everyone down the rope before the dragons return!" orders Zarkon.

Turn to page 85.

You step as far back on the platform as you can, take a short run, and leap out into space.

You don't quite make it.

As you plummet downward, the dragon—with Zarkon and Virgana still aboard—swoops down and catches you in its mouth. With just enough pressure, the dragon's ghastly teeth hold you without hurting you. You are transported gently down to the ground and released. At the same time Zarkon and Virgana slide down the side of the dragon's head to safety. Then the dragon roars off.

Zarkon hands the dragon staff back to you. "It's not wise for me as a good wizard to hold this staff too long," he says. "Controlling dragons is one of the evil arts. *You*, however, can do it for a short time and come away unscathed."

Turn to page 91.

"Roping down from above seems the safest," you say.

You start up the path toward the top of the cliff, high over the waterfall. You lead the way and get to the top well ahead of the others.

You get slightly dizzy looking down, so you decide to look toward the top of the mountain until the others catch up with you. As you look up, you notice a tower high on the mountain. And on top of the tower—so distant that it is a mere speck—you see a face. There is something about it . . . The face seems to grow in your mind until you can see nothing else. Two eyes . . . They overpower you.

You stagger backward. Your foot slips on the edge of the cliff and you hurtle into space. Desperately, Zarkon shoots his magic rope at you as you fall. But the rope misses. You hit the surface of the lake—and vanish forever into its deep waters.

The End

You follow the river downstream for quite a distance. The light grows a bit stronger in the tunnel. Then, far ahead, you see a bright spot of light. It must be the place where the river leaves the mountain. You decide to rest for a bit and then continue down to the exit.

Turn to page 95.

You wave the dragon staff in the air. The dragons move like gigantic kites across the sky—as if they were controlled by strings attached to the staff.

High above, looking over the top edge of the tower, are the tiny faces of Tarlane and Mordana. Then you hear them scream as one of the dragons crashes headlong into the tower and sends it crashing to the ground.

You run to search the rubble for Tarlane and Mordana, but they are nowhere to be found.

Turn to page 100.

"I've always wanted to climb a balcony," you say nervously. Zarkon tosses his rope up to it, and one by one you climb onto it. The balcony leads into a small, square room with metal walls. A large, round mirror is set into one side. Below the mirror are some small circles with arrows in them.

"This *is* curious," says Zarkon, walking over to the mirror. He presses a spot on the wall at the side of the mirror, and the mirror begins to light up from behind. Then a moving picture of two dragons fighting furiously in the sky appears on it.

"Those must be the two dragons I rousted out from the den," says Zarkon. "Now we are seeing them outside in the sky."

"Is this a kind of crystal ball?" Virgana asks.

"Sort of," answers Zarkon, "but not quite. It's hard to explain the difference."

Gnali, Virgana, and Zarkon stand watching the dragon fight. You look around and notice a small alcove in one corner. You step inside to investigate.

"Quick!" Zarkon shouts to you. "Get out of there before—"

You start to jump out, but you are not fast enough. Suddenly, a door snaps shut, trapping you inside. Almost instantly the alcove, or whatever it is you are trapped in, zips upward at a great speed. Your stomach feels as if it has dropped to your knees.

Turn to page 22.

"I don't like the looks of that," you say. "We haven't got much of a chance out here in the open if they attack us."

"Don't worry," says Zarkon. "I recognize my friend Valerian in the lead. He's the captain of the king's guard."

The horsemen gallop up to you and dismount. "Zarkon, I'm glad that I found you," Valerian says. "The king requests your urgent return to the castle."

"But I'm on an important mission," says Zarkon.

"Prince Rupert has fallen ill," Valerian says.

"Again!" Zarkon exclaims.

"This time it appears more serious than the times before," says Valerian. "Your presence always seems to cure him."

"I know," Zarkon says with a sigh. "I guess I'll have to go. He is, after all, the heir to the throne. Half of your party will return with me to the castle. The other half will provide safe escort for my companions to a point high on the mountain."

"I'm sorry, Zarkon," Valerian says, "but my orders do not include—"

Zarkon raises his staff and glowers.

"I advise you to do as I say," he commands. "You know how I get when I'm mad."

Turn to page 61.

You sit down on the ledge with your back against the wall. Then you notice a whistling sound above you. There's a hole of some sort in the wall over your head. You stand up again and are just about to investigate when you're startled by a face peering at you from a short distance away. It is the face of a dwarf.

Turn to page 67.

As you fly over the edge of the tower Mordana lets go of you. You slip down and grab her ankles. Above you, Mordana spreads out her arms and her cape fills with air, slowing your descent to the ground. The two of you land with a crash at the bottom of the tower. You are shaken up, but otherwise all right. You run away from the tower as fast as you can.

In the distance you see that the dragon has set Zarkon and Virgana down on the ground. Then it flies up into the air and blasts the tower with its flaming breath. The top of the tower explodes in flame and smoke, hurling huge stones in all directions. You are already running toward Virgana and Zarkon. You reach them safely through the thick pall of black smoke.

When the smoke clears, there is no trace of Tarlane or Mordana, and in the confusion the dragon staff has disappeared.

You, Zarkon, and Virgana hike back down the mountain to town. For the time being you've had your fill of treasure hunting.

The End

Zarkon, Gnali, and you make your way back along the river. Suddenly, you are surrounded by small figures with crossbows.

"Gnali!" one of them shouts. "You've come back!"

The dwarfs lead you to their banquet hall, where they prepare a feast in your honor. Zarkon, having finished his first mission, vanishes back into the mountain.

Later, when you tell the dwarfs of your quest for dragon treasure, they take you to a small observation hole high above the dragons' den. You feast your eyes on the treasure that is piled on the floor way below. But you also see the size of the dragons guarding it. You are quite satisfied when the dwarfs give you a purse full of gold nuggets and lead you safely out of the mountain.

The End

You dive into the deep water and start swimming for the ledge. The current sweeps you downstream. Finally you reach the other side, but the ledge is higher above the water than you thought. You have to try several times before you manage to pull yourself up.

You sit there for a while, catching your breath. You have to decide which direction you will take. If you follow the river downstream, it should lead you out of the mountain and to safety. On the other hand, going upriver may lead you to new dangers—but it may also lead you to treasure.

If you go downstream, turn to page 90.

If you go upstream, turn to page 104.

You race back to the other part of the mine. You get there just as they are finishing the wall, sealing off the dragon run. You barely manage to squeeze through.

You are supposed to be released today, but you've done your job as water bearer too well. You have become indispensable to the operation of the mine. Your term is extended to a year; later to five years; and after that to life.

The End

"Over here!" Virgana shouts. "It looks as if one of the tower blocks has caved in the entrance to Tarlane's quarters." Sure enough, in front of you is a large hole in the ground and a ladder leading down.

Slowly the three of you descend. Inside you find Tarlane's treasure rooms, filled with sacks of jewels and gold coins that were taken as ransom from the dragon-threatened kingdoms.

"There's enough treasure here to last us forever!" shouts Virgana.

Later, with Zarkon's help, you find the combination of bumps on the dragon staff that sends the dragons back to their den and makes them sleep. Then you seal the dragon staff in a deep vault and hope that the dragons will stay sleeping under the mountain forever.

The End

"Let's try the tunnel," you say. "At least we won't have to do any hard climbing."

The three of you go into the tunnel. The air inside is very warm. Soon it becomes hotter and hotter. Finally you have to stop.

"Going this way was probably a mistake," you admit. "We should turn back."

Just then a loud roar from behind you fills the tunnel! A blast of flame follows.

"What is that?" asks Virgana in a worried voice.

"A fire lizard," says Zarkon. "They are not as large as dragons, but they can be just as deadly. As you've seen, they can breathe fire. Unlike dragons, they are unable to fly. However, even the smallest fire lizard can outrun a horse."

Another roar—much closer this time—fills the tunnel. Whatever it is, it's coming in your direction fast! The three of you dash down the tunnel in the opposite direction.

Turn to page 55.

"Let's go through the door!" you say.

The four of you push open the heavy dragon door and peer into a dimly lit chamber. It's full of baby dragons dozing on top of one another.

"We'll have to go through," says Zarkon, "but be careful."

One by one you pick your way through the chamber, cautiously stepping between tails and over toes. Just as you pass the last dragon, its eyes blink open. Instantly you clamp your hands around its jaws just in time to muffle its shriek. As it squirms, you hang on desperately. In a few minutes the baby dragon tires. You know that if you let it go, it will alert the others. You have no choice. Holding the dragon tightly in your arms, you carry it out of the nursery and into a tunnel where the others are waiting.

"You wanted treasure," Zarkon says with a smile. "Well, you've got it and more!" Gnali and Virgana can hardly contain their amusement.

"It's easy for you to laugh," you say, sourly. "You don't have to carry this guy." Turning, you stride down the tunnel that leads safely out of the mountain.

The End

You walk upstream for what must be miles. Then the ledge ends at a small tunnel. You walk forward into the tunnel, even though you have to stoop over to do it.

You come out into a large cavern. There is a faint light—just enough to see by. On the other side of the cavern you can make out an enormous, closed gate. You head toward it. But before you reach the gate you find yourself surrounded by dozens of small creatures. You blink and look again. They are dwarfs.

Each of the dwarfs is armed with a small crossbow. You raise your arm and start to speak—but you don't get a chance to finish. At a signal, all the dwarfs fire at you. And though their arrows are small, they are deadly. Too bad!

The End

You watch the space between you and the dragon grow wider as you turn and look back at the door. The hinges give way, and the door comes crashing out. You stand there facing Tarlane and Mordana. Tarlane looks at you and then at Zarkon on the dragon's head several feet out from the edge of the tower. Tarlane has some sort of metal object cradled in his hand. He starts to point it at Zarkon. Quick as a flash you bat his hand aside. The object makes a loud noise as it goes flying off into space. Tarlane looks at his empty hand in amazement for a second. Immediately you tackle him and throw him to the tower platform.

Turn to page 113.

Taking the sword might be too dangerous. But then again . . . You are about to change your mind when you hear someone coming. Quickly, you hide behind a heavy screen.

A man and a woman enter the room. They talk briefly and then the woman leaves. The man walks over and stands in front of the screen where you are hiding. Somehow he knows you are behind it! A strange metal object is in his hand. A weapon! You push the screen, trying to knock him over, but he jumps to one side. *Bang!* The noise seems to come from the object in his hand. At almost the same time, something knocks you backward. You feel a terrible pain in your chest.

You've been shot in the sixth century—hundreds of years before the invention of the gun.

The End

You are at home anywhere, so banishment doesn't sound too bad. At least it's better than the salt mines. You and Virgana's friend are escorted under guard to the border of the kingdom and are warned not to come back.

There's plenty of treasure in the world, and you will find lots of it in other places. But you will always wonder about the treasure of Dragon Mountain.

The End

The three of you race for the tower. Frantically you search around the base, but there is no way in. The black shapes are now clearly the hideous forms of dragons. A dozen of them close in and begin circling the tower.

"What'll we do now?" Gnali asks in a shaky voice.

Before you can answer, a huge blast of flame whips across the mountaintop. When the smoke clears, only the scorched earth remains around the blackened stone tower.

The End

"The staff is too close to Tarlane for me to grab it without being seen," you say.

Tarlane starts singing in the shower—at the top of his voice and off-tune.

"If I know Mordana," says Zarkon, "she won't be able to stand Tarlane's singing. She'll probably go to another part of the quarters until he's finished. Let's try to sneak out."

Sure enough, when you get to the other room Mordana is nowhere to be seen. You tiptoe silently down one of the side corridors and come to a heavy iron door.

"I wonder if it's locked," you whisper.

"We won't know unless we try it," says Virgana with a grin.

Carefully, you lift the latch and pull. The door swings silently open.

Turn to page 60.

Meanwhile, Mordana and Zarkon are having a different kind of battle. Their burning stares meet midway in the air—and a crackling ball of flame forms there. Zarkon is struggling to control the dragon with the dragon staff as the flaming ball creeps closer to him.

Tarlane struggles free of your grasp and dives back down the tower stairs. You grab Mordana from behind, just as the ball of flame is about to envelop Zarkon's head. The flame evaporates— you've saved Zarkon from a fiery death. Then the dragon, with Zarkon and Virgana, flies off.

Mordana whirls around to give *you* her flaming whammy. But before she can, you duck down under her line of sight and give her a big shove backward. At the same moment, Mordana grabs hold of you—and both of you sail off the edge of the tower platform.

Turn to page 96.

Zarkon gives a long, loud whistle. Soon you see more black spots coming from over the mountaintops.

"Terrific," says Virgana. "Here come more dragons. We're done for now."

"No," says Zarkon, "they are friends."

And you can see that Zarkon is right. They aren't dragons in the sky but eagles. Huge ones!

"The eagles are enemies of the dragons," Zarkon explains, "and will aid those in danger from the dragons. Stand by the edge here and be ready to grab on to them."

Sure enough, only seconds later, three eagles swoop down. Their strong wings beat rhythmically in the air as they carry the three of you safely back to town.

Later, Zarkon treats you and Virgana to dinner at the inn.

"Tomorrow we'll go back to the cave and try to find out if Gnali is all right," he says.

You and Virgana agree. You don't realize it now, but many adventures still lie ahead of you— inside Dragon Mountain.

The End

You go back, pick one of the tunnels, and enter it. Soon you see a red glow up ahead. You come out of the tunnel—into a scene that reminds you of pictures of hell! Bubbling springs of molten rock are all around you. A heavy sulfur smell fills the air. And it is very, very hot. Down below in a deep chasm, a glowing stream of lava flows slowly. A narrow stone arch stretches over the fiery stream.

Turn to page 75.

The cabinet doors open again. Outside is a room much like the one inside Dragon Mountain, but much larger. A group of men all dressed like Tarlane stand there. Tarlane jumps to his feet.

"Where are the dragon eggs you promised us?" one of the men asks Tarlane in a threatening tone. "Time is running out. The enemy planes must feel the talons of the dragons."

"I . . . I couldn't bring them this time," Tarlane says. "This intruder set back my plans."

"Then you will pay," says the man, pointing at you.

All of the men take out strange weapons like the one Tarlane had tried to use against you. They point them at you. As if on signal, they all fire at the same time.

The End

ABOUT THE AUTHOR

RICHARD BRIGHTFIELD is a graduate of Johns Hopkins University, where he studied biology, psychology, and archaeology. For many years he worked as a graphic designer at Columbia University. He has written *Secret of the Pyramids*, *The Phantom Submarine*, and *The Curse of Batterslea Hall* in the Choose Your Own Adventure series and has coauthored more than a dozen game books with his wife, Glory. The Brightfields and their daughter, Savitri, live in Gardiner, New York.

ABOUT THE ILLUSTRATOR

PAUL ABRAMS has worked as an artist for Marvel Comics and *Heavy Metal* magazine. He has also taught art professionally and, in addition, was a rock musician for several years. Mr. Abrams lives in New Paltz, New York.

CHOOSE YOUR OWN ADVENTURE

BANTAM
SHOP·AT·HOME
C·A·T·A·L·O·G

Shop at home
for quality childrens books
and save money, too.

Now you can order books for the whole family from Bantam's latest listing of hundreds of titles including many fine children's books. *And* this special offer gives you an opportunity to purchase a Bantam book for only 50¢. Here's how:

By ordering any five books at the regular price per order, you can also choose any other single book listed (up to $4.95 value) for just 50¢. Some restrictions do apply, so for further details send for Bantam's listing of titles today.